ZION
NATIONAL PARK
ACTIVITY BOOK

PUZZLES, MAZES, GAMES, AND MORE ABOUT ZION NATIONAL PARK

NATIONAL PARKS ACTIVITIES SERIES

ZION NATIONAL PARK ACTIVITY BOOK

Copyright 2021
Published by Little Bison Press

The author acknowledges that the land on which Zion National Park is located are the traditional lands of Southern Paiute and Pueblos Tribes.

For more free national parks activities, visit
www.littlebisonpress.com

About Zion National Park

Zion National Park is located in the state of Utah. The park is famous for its scenic canyons. The Zion Canyon was carved over millions of years by the Virgin River and is approximately two thousand feet deep. Zion harbors over a thousand plant species that allow a wide variety of wildlife to flourish! The park is a popular bird-watching destination with almost three hundred species, including the largest flying bird in North America, the endangered California Condor.

Many visitors stay into the evening to view the glowing colors of the sunset light up Zion's cliffs. Because of the quality of starry nights and protected night skies, Zion is a designated International Dark Sky Park. If you are able to spend the night in one of the campgrounds, you may get a spectacular view of the star-filled night sky above the jagged silhouette of cliffs.

Zion National Park is famous for:
- scenic canyons
- hiking trails, rock climbing, and backpacking
- breathtaking sunsets and stargazing

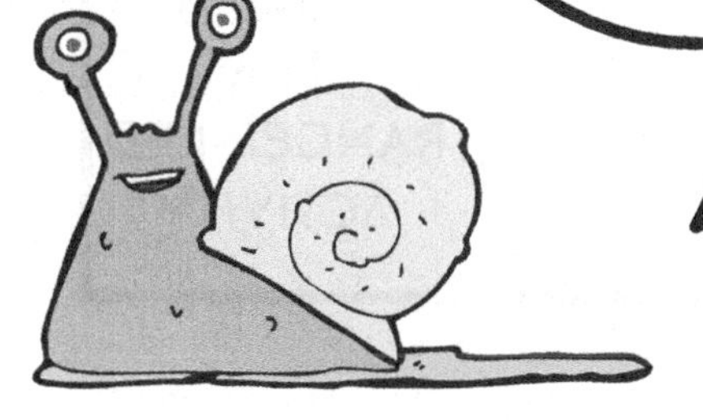

Zion Bingo

Let's play bingo! Cross off each box you are able to during your visit to the national park. Try to get a bingo down, across, or diagonally. If you can't visit the park, use the bingo board to plan your perfect trip.

Pick out some activities you would want to do during your visit. What would you do first? How long would you spend there? What animals would you try to see?

DRINK EXTRA WATER	SEE HOODOOS	IDENTIFY A TREE	TAKE A PICTURE AT AN OVERLOOK	WATCH A MOVIE AT THE VISITORS CENTER
GO FOR A HIKE	LEARN ABOUT THE INDIGENOUS PEOPLE WHO LIVE IN THIS AREA	WITNESS A SUNRISE OR SUNSET	OBSERVE THE NIGHT SKIES	GO STARGAZING
HEAR A BIRD CALL	WADE IN THE RIVER	FREE SPACE	LEARN ABOUT THE VIRGIN RIVER	VISIT A RANGER STATION
PICK UP TEN PIECES OF TRASH	GO CAMPING	SEE A MULE DEER	VISIT THE ZION LODGE	SPOT A BIRD OF PREY
LEARN ABOUT THE GEOLOGY OF ZION	VISIT THE NARROWS	HAVE A PICNIC	SPOT SOME ANIMAL TRACKS	PARTICIPATE IN A RANGER-LED ACTIVITY

The National Park Logo

The National Park System has over 400 units in the US. Just like Zion National Park, each location is unique or special in some way. The areas include other national parks, historic sites, monuments, seashores, and other recreation areas.

Each element of the National Park emblem represents something that the National Park Service protects. Fill in each blank below to show what each symbol represents.

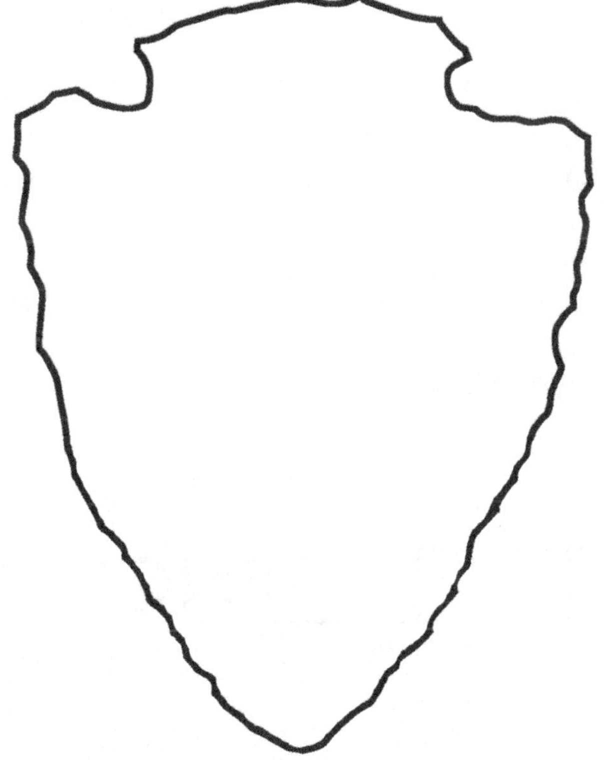

> ### WORD BANK:
>
> MOUNTAINS, ARROWHEAD, BISON, SEQUOIA TREE, WATER

This represents all plants. ______________________

This represents all animals. ______________________

This represents the landscapes. ______________________

This represents the waters protected by the park service. ______________________

This represents the historical and archeological values. ______________________

Now it's your turn! Pretend you are designing a new national park. Add elements to the design that represent the things your park protects.

What is the name of your park?

Describe why you included the symbols that you included. What do they mean?

Things to Do Jumble

Unscramble the letters to uncover activities you can do while in Zion National Park. Hint: each one ends in -ing.

1. SARTGZA ☐☐☐☐☐☐☐ING

2. KHI ☐☐☐ING

3. RIBD ☐☐☐☐ING

4. MAPC ☐☐☐☐ING

5. KINICPC ☐☐☐☐☐☐☐ING

6. ESSTEIGH ☐☐☐☐☐☐☐☐ING

7. RABEHOSRCKID ☐☐☐☐☐☐☐☐☐☐☐☐ING

Word Bank

birding
reading
camping
stargazing
horseback riding
hiking
fishing
singing
yelling
sightseeing
picnicking

Staying Safe in the Sun

It is important to take precautions to stay safe outdoors, especially when it is very hot outside. When someone gets overheated or dehydrated, they may feel sick or even require medical attention.

Use the cryptogram below to decode three tips on how to prevent heat-related illnesses. You may need to do some math to figure out the answers.

T _ _ _ _   _ _ _ _ _ _ _   _ _ _   _ _ _ _
12 5 12/2 50   30 21 50 5 2x3 36   3x4 27   21 50 6x6 12

_ _   _ _ _   _ _ _ _ _ .
99 10   15-3 4 50   36 7-3 5 1 50

_ _ _ _   H _ _ _ _ _ _ _ _   _ _
36 12 1x5 18   4 2x9 1 21 5 12 50 8-7   30 18

_ _ _ _ _ _ _ _ _   _ _ _ _   _ _   _ _ _ _ _ .
1 21 99 10 6 33x3 10 75   35 3x9 12 36   27 5x5   18/2 5 12 50 21

_ _ A _   _ _ _ _ _ _ _ _ _ _   _ _ _
9 50 12-7 21   36 3 10 36 15 21 5x10 50 10   5 10 12-11

_ _ _ - _ _ _ _ _ _ _ _ _ _
36 3 10   8 7x3 27 12 50 15 9+3 99 80 50

_ _ _ _ _ I N G .
15 35 27 12 2x2 99 10 75

a	b	c	d	e	f	g	h	i	j	k	l	m	n	o
5	30	15	1	50	25	75	4	99	20	6	35	49	10	27

p	q	r	s	t	u	v	w	x	y	z
8	16	21	36	12	3	80	9	40	18	7

Go Birdwatching at Watchman Trail

Camping Packing List

What should you take with you when you go camping? Pretend you are in charge of your family camping trip. Make a list of what you would need to be safe and comfortable on an overnight excursion. Some considerations are listed on the side.

1.

2.

3.

4.

5.

6.

7.

8.

9.

10.

11.

12.

13.

14.

15.

16.

- What will you eat at every meal?

- What will the weather be like?

- Where will you sleep?

- What will you do during your free time?

- How luxurious do you want camp to be?

- How will you cook?

- How will you see at night?

- How will you dispose of trash?

- What might you need in case of emergencies?

Zion National Park has 3 developed campgrounds. People can also get permits to camp in the backcountry.

See page 20 for more information about what this means!

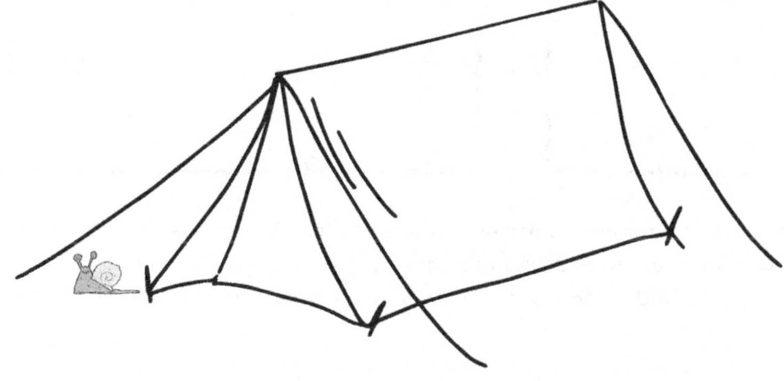

Zion National Park

Date:

Season:

Who I went with:

Which entrance:

How was your experience? Write a few sentences about your trip. Where did you stay? What did you do? What was your favorite activity? If you haven't visited the park yet, write a paragraph pretending that you did.

STAMPS

Many national parks and monuments have cancellation stamps for visitors to use. These rubber stamps record the date and location that you visited. Many people collect the markings as a free souvenir. Check with a ranger to see where you can find a stamp during your visit. If you aren't able to find one, you can draw your own.

Where is the Park?

Zion National Park is in the northwest United States. It is located in Utah. The nickname for Utah is the Beehive State. Can you find Utah on the map?

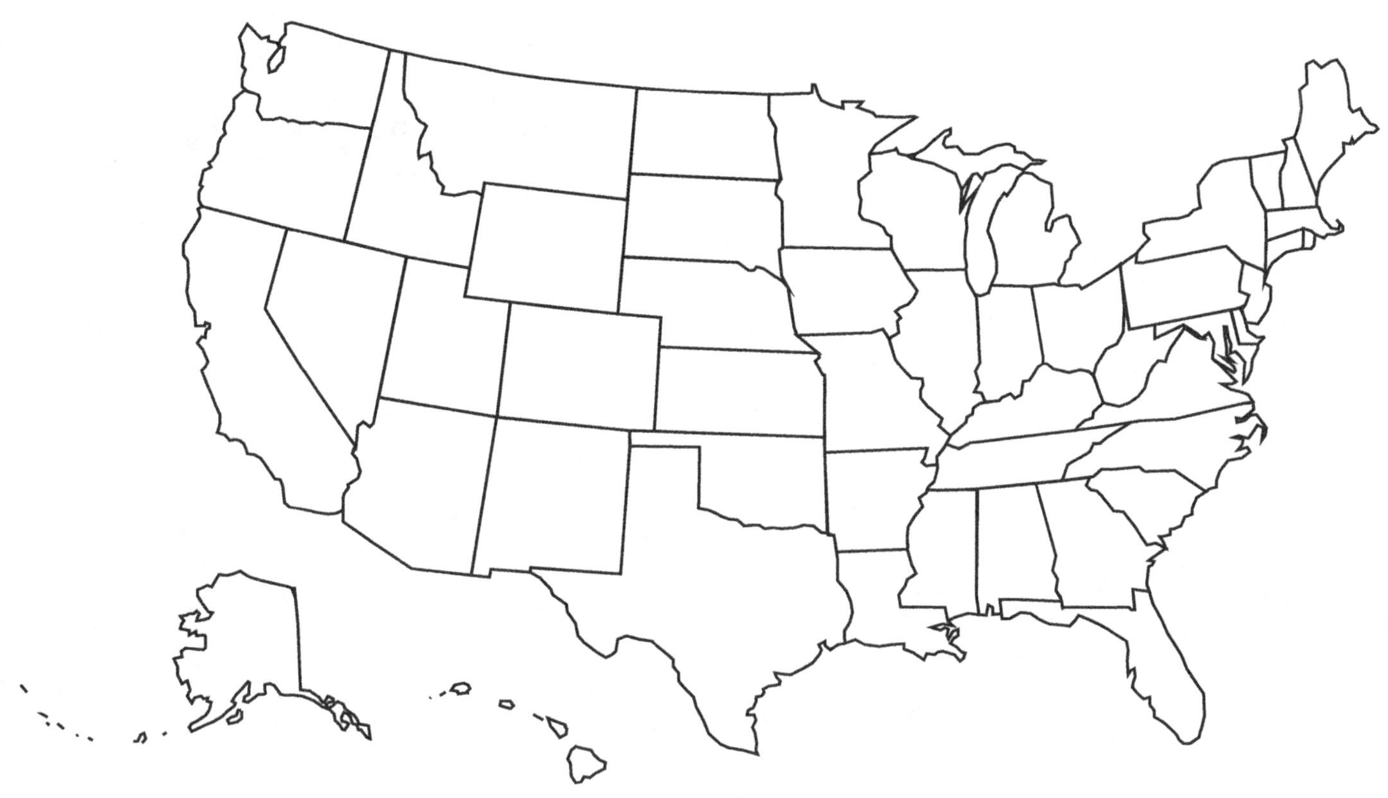

Utah

Look at the shape of Utah. Can you find it on the map? If you are from the US, can you find your home state? Color Utah red. Color every state that touches Utah green. Put a star on the map where you live. Color the remaining states any way you wish.

Connect the Dots #1

Connect the dots to figure out what this tiny critter is. There are three types of these that live in Zion National Park.

Their heart rate can reach as high as 1,260 beats per minute and a breathing rate of 250 breaths per minute. Have you ever measured your breathing rate? Ask a friend or family member to set a timer for 60 seconds. Once they say "go," try to breathe normally. Count each breath until they say "stop." How do your breaths per minute compare to hummingbirds?

____

____

Whiptail lizards are relatively small lizards with long tails. All whiptails are females as they reproduce asexually.

Cottontail rabbits typically have a stubby white-colored tail. One of the most common predators of cottontails are birds of prey.

Who Lives Here?

Below are 9 plants and animals that live in the park.
Use the word bank to fill in the clues below.

(Puzzle grid with acrostic spine reading S-O-U-T-H-W-E-S-T)

WORD BANK:

CHEATGRASS, GOPHER SNAKE, BOBCAT, CANYON WREN, MULE DEER, PRICKLY PEAR, COTTONTAIL, OSPREY, WHIPTAIL

Bighorn sheep are named for the large horns grown by the males of the species. In Zion, they can often be seen in areas near the east side of the park.

The California Condor is one of the rarest birds in the world.
They were almost extinct, but conservation efforts have helped increase their population numbers. If you see one perched, look at it but don't approach it.
They are curious birds!

Common Names
vs.
Scientific Names

A common name of an organism is a name that is based on everyday language. You have heard the common names of plants, animals, and other living things on tv, in books, and at school. Common names can also be referred to as "English" names, popular names, or farmer's names. Common names can vary from place to place. The word for a particular tree may be one thing, but that same tree has a different name in another country. Common names can even vary from region to region, even in the same country.

Scientific names, or Latin names, are given to organisms to make it possible to have uniform names for the same species. Scientific names are in Latin. You may have heard plants or animals referred to by their scientific name or parts of their scientific names. Latin names are also called "binomial nomenclature," which refers to a two-part naming system. The first part of the name – the generic name – refers to the genus to which the species belongs. The second part of the name, the specific name, identifies the species. For example, Tyrannosaurus rex is an example of a widely known scientific name.

LATIN NAME = GENUS + SPECIES

Bighorn Sheep = Ovis canadensis

Black Bear = Ursus americanus

Find the Match!
Common Names and Latin Names

Match the common name to the scientific name for each animal. The first one is done for you. Use clues on the page before and after this one to complete the matches.

Bighorn Sheep	Haliaeetus leucocephalus
Two-needle Piñon	Ursus americanus
Cheatgrass	Pandion haliaetus
American Black Bear	Opuntia engelmannii
Great Horned Owl	Pinus edulis
Bald Eagle	Aspidoscelis uniparens
Osprey	Bubo virginianus
Prickly Pear	Ovis canadensis
Whiptail	Bromus tectorum

Bald Eagle

Haliaeetus leucocephalus

Osprey
Pandion haliaetus

Two-needle Piñon
Pinus edulis

Great Horned Owl
Bubo virginianus

Some plants and animals that live in Zion

Prickly Pear
Opuntia engelmannii

Cheatgrass
Bromus tectorum

Whiptail
Aspidoscelis uniparens

Color the Cliffs of Zion

The Ten Essentials

Careful preparation and knowledge are key to a successful adventure into Zion National Park's backcountry.

The ten essentials are a list of things that are important to have when you go for longer hikes. If you go on a hike in the <u>backcountry,</u> it is especially important that you have everything you need in case of an emergency. If you get lost or something unforeseen happens, it is good to be prepared to survive until help finds you.

The ten essentials list was developed in the 1930s by an outdoors group called the Mountaineers. Over time and technological advancements, this list has evolved. Can you identify all the things on the current list? Circle each of the "essentials" and cross out everything that doesn't make the cut.

fire: matches, lighter, tinder, and/or stove	a pint of milk	extra money	headlamp, plus extra batteries	extra clothes
extra water	a dog	Polaroid camera	bug net	lightweight games, like a deck of cards
extra food	a roll of duct tape	shelter	sun protection, such as sunglasses, sun-protective clothes, and sunscreen	knife, plus a gear repair kit
a mirror	navigation: map, compass, altimeter, GPS device, or satellite messenger	first aid kit	extra flip-flops	entertainment, such as video games or books

Backcountry - a remote, undeveloped rural area.

Take a Hike

Go for a hike with your friends or family. If you aren't able to visit Zion National Park, go for a walk in a park near where you live. Read through the prompts before your walk and finish the activities after you return.

Draw something you saw that moves:

Draw something you saw when you looked up:

Draw something you saw that grows out of the ground:

Draw a picture of your favorite part of the walk:

Connect the Dots #2

This animal lives in almost every state in the US, including the national park. They are nocturnal, more active at night, and sleep during the day. They are omnivorous eaters, meaning they eat both plants and animals.

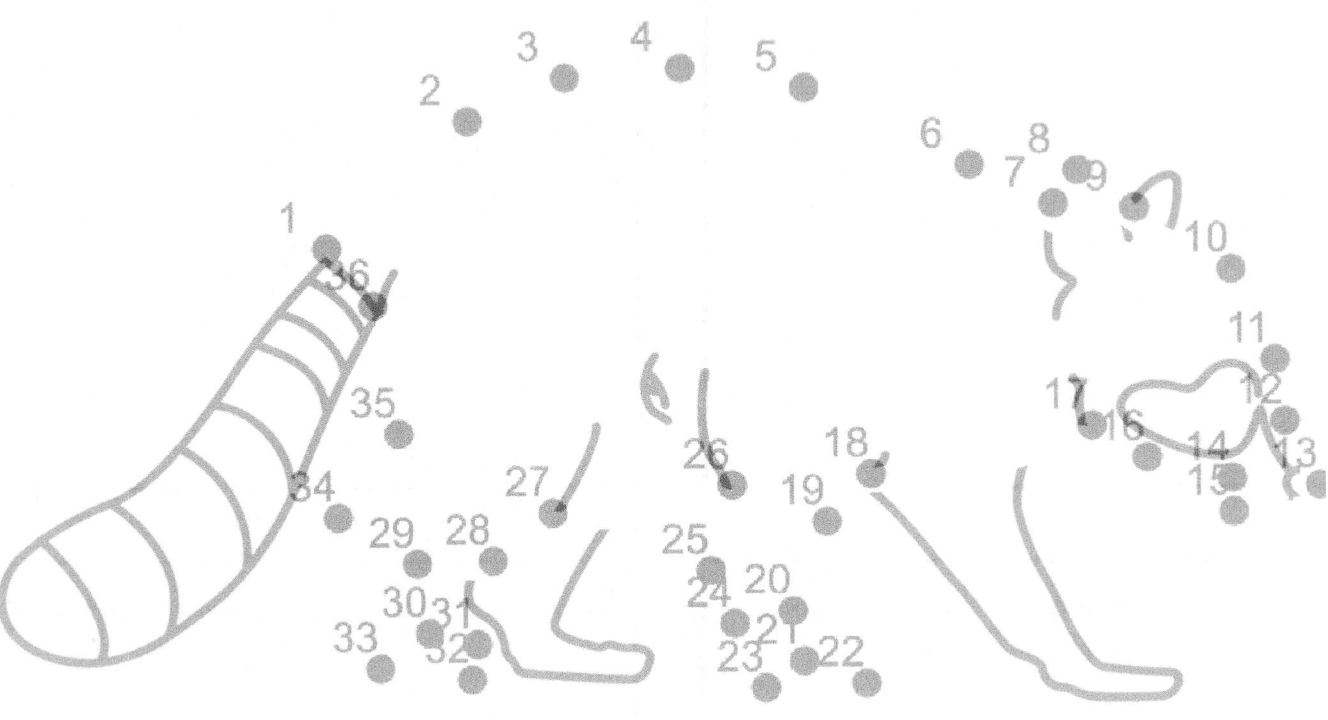

Are you an omnivore like a raccoon? An herbivore only eats plant foods. A carnivore only eats meat. An omnivore eats both. What type of eater are you? Write down some of your favorite foods to back up your answer.

____

____

LISTEN CAREFULLY

Visitors to Zion National Park may hear different noises from those they hear at home. Try this activity to experience this for yourself!

First, find a place outside where it is comfortable to sit or stand for a few minutes. You can do this by yourself or with a friend or family member. Once you have a good spot, close your eyes and listen. Be quiet for one minute and pay attention to what you are hearing. List some of the sounds you have heard in one of the two boxes below:

NATURAL SOUNDS
MADE BY ANIMALS, TREES OR PLANTS, THE WIND, ETC

HUMAN-MADE SOUNDS
MADE BY PEOPLE, MACHINES, ETC

ONCE YOU ARE BACK AT HOME, TRY REPEATING YOUR EXPERIMENT:

NATURAL SOUNDS
MADE BY ANIMALS, TREES OR PLANTS, THE WIND, ETC

HUMAN-MADE SOUNDS
MADE BY PEOPLE, MACHINES, ETC

WHERE DID YOU HEAR MORE NATURAL SOUNDS? ______________________

WHERE DID YOU HEAR MORE HUMAN SOUNDS? ______________________

Bird Scavenger Hunt 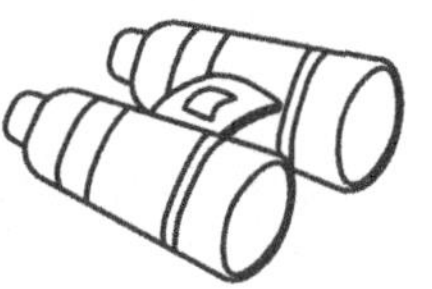

Zion National Park is a great place to go birdwatching. You don't have to be able to identify different species of birds in order to have fun. Open your eyes and tune in your ears. Check off as many birds on this list as you can.

☐ A colorful bird	☐ A big bird
☐ A brown bird	☐ A small bird
☐ A bird in a tree	☐ A hopping bird
☐ A bird with long tail feathers	☐ A flying bird
☐ A bird making noise	☐ A bird's nest
☐ A bird eating or hunting	☐ A bird's footprint on the ground
☐ A bird with spots	☐ A bird with stripes somewhere on it

What was the easiest bird on the list to find? What was the hardest?
Why do you think that was?

____

____

____

Zion Word Search 

Angels Landing is one of the most famous hikes in all of the National Park System. It is a trail on a fin-like cliff that is steep and strenuous. Its name allegedly comes from Methodist minister Frederick Vining Fisher who joked that only an angel could land there. Now thousands of people attempt this hike every year!

1. Narrows
2. Kolob
3. sunset
4. rafting
5. southwest
6. Lava Point
7. flash flood
8. lodge
9. yucca
10. juniper
11. Paiute
12. Mormon
13. homestead
14. plateau
15. sandstone
16. condor
17. shuttle
18. Angels Landing

```
H M R E G N I M O Y W R M D F
L A V A P O I N T R O A O A L
O L N F P I T H F U L F S G A
S C H G O L I C E L T T U H S
L O D G E Y A T E S E I N G H
V N D S L L G T B I S N S E F
P D H O M E S T E A D G E N L
E O M A R N O L E A E T T R O
R R P T O O T P A I U T E C O
K S Y M H E K R T N N A S A D
L G R A F E N O T S D N A S A
A O D H R F A G L K H I O P R
M I E W I A R O I O T I N I C
J U N I P E R N N A B C D G H
R M N L E R O D S A C C U Y O
A S Q U I R W E L E R A M E N
O C R T R A S O U T H W E S T
B J A C K N B R I V E R A D M
```

Find the Match!
What are Baby Animals Called?

Match the animal to its baby. The first one is done for you.

Elk	eaglet
Bald Eagle	calf
Little Brown Bat	snakelets
Striped Skunk	pup
Great Horned Owl	owlet
Western Toad	kit
Mountain Lion	tadpole
Garter snake	kitten

Rain, Rain, Rain

If it rains while you are visiting Zion National Park, you can do this activity during your trip. If you don't get any rain while you are there, you can follow the same instructions next time it rains where you live.

Go outside into the rain. Use all of your senses as you complete the boxes below. You can use words, drawings, or both.

Sit as still as you can and listen to the rain. How does it make you feel?

Look straight up at the sky and let the raindrops fall on your face. Close your eyes. How does it feel?

Watch where the rain goes. Pay attention to the different surfaces the rain lands on. Which surfaces absorb the rain, and which surfaces cause the rain to run off or pool?

Are there any animals or bugs out enjoying the rain? Do you think the plants are enjoying the rain?

The Perfect Picnic Spot

Fill in the blanks on this page without looking at the full story. Once you have each line filled out, use the words you've chosen to complete the story on the next page.

EMOTION ____

FOOD ____

SOMETHING SWEET ____

STORE ____

MODE OF TRANSPORTATION ____

NOUN ____

SOMETHING ALIVE ____

SAUCE ____

PLURAL VEGETABLES ____

ADJECTIVE ____

PLURAL BODY PART ____

ANIMAL ____

PLURAL FRUIT ____

PLACE ____

SOMETHING TALL ____

COLOR ____

ADJECTIVE ____

NOUN ____

A DIFFERENT ANIMAL ____

FAMILY MEMBER #1 ____

FAMILY MEMBER #2 ____

VERB THAT ENDS IN -ING ____

A DIFFERENT FOOD ____

The Perfect Picnic Spot

Use the words from the previous page to complete a silly story.

When my family suggested having our lunch at the Grotto Picnic Area, I was

_________. I love eating my ______ outside! I knew we had picked up a
EMOTION · FOOD

box of ______ from the _________ for after lunch, my favorite. We drove up
SOMETHING SWEET · STORE

to the area and I jumped out of the _________. "I will find the perfect spot for
MODE OF TRANSPORTATION

a picnic!" I grabbed a ______ for us to sit on, and I ran off. I passed a picnic
NOUN

table, but it was covered with _________ so we couldn't sit there. The next
SOMETHING ALIVE

picnic table looked okay, but there were smears of _______ and pieces of
SAUCE

_________ everywhere. The people that were there before must have been
PLURAL VEGETABLES

______! I gritted my _______ together and kept walking down the path,
ADJECTIVE · PLURAL BODY PART

determined to find the perfect spot. I wanted a table with a good view of the

cliffs. Why was this so hard? If we were lucky, I might even get to see ______
ANIMAL

eating some ______ on the cliffside. They don't have those in _______ where I
PLURAL FRUIT · PLACE

am from. I walked down a little hill and there it was, the perfect spot! The trees

towered overhead and looked as tall as _________. The patch of grass was a
SOMETHING TALL

beautiful _______ color. The ______ flowers were growing on
COLOR · ADJECTIVE

the side of a _______. I looked across the cliff edge and even saw a
NOUN

_________ on the edge of a rock. I looked back to see my __________ and
DIFFERENT ANIMAL · FAMILY MEMBER #1

__________ _________ a picnic basket. "I hope you brought plenty of
FAMILY MEMBER #2 · VERB THAT ENDS IN ING

_______, I'm starving!"
A DIFFERENT FOOD

Hike to a Hoodoo

DID YOU KNOW?
Hoodoos are tall, thin rocks that protrude from the bottom of a basin. Have you seen any in the park?

Utah Word Search

Words may be horizontal, vertical, diagonal, or they might even be backwards!

1. osprey
2. Utah
3. southwest
4. canyon
5. explore
6. reptile
7. dry
8. desert
9. hiking
10. rocks
11. Salt Lake City
12. geology
13. pinyon pine
14. pine nuts
15. cliffs
16. beehive
17. arid
18. cactus

```
C W S O U T H W E S T L O W K
H T A A K I L O C H E L A N J
T G E O L O G Y C C L B A P E
P M P A Y T R S C E R L H L X
I I A D R A L L O E I U I A P
N O N D D I R A D C T T K S L
Y E S E E H E K K B P R I C O
O L B A N U I E G E N E N A R
N E H S G U L O R E C D G D E
P C I C A C T U S H P I O E A
I T A L C H I S O I K E T S N
N R N I K O E I O V O K I Y E
E I O F H Z D E S E R T L G W
J C G F L O V E P O O R V E H
N I L S K H I N R O C K S E A
X T A I A E E G E Z E P R N L
H T D T O E N O Y N A C C I E
U J U O S N E D N Y M A L A Z
```

Leave No Trace Quiz

Leave No Trace is a concept that helps people make decisions during outdoor recreation that protects the environment. There are seven principles that guide us when we spend time outdoors, whether you are in a national park or not. Are you an expert in Leave No Trace? Take this quiz and find out!

1. How can you plan ahead and prepare to ensure you have the best experience you can in the national park?
    a. Make sure you stop by the ranger station for a map and to ask about current conditions.
    b. Just wing it! You will know the best trail when you see it.
    c. Stick to your plan, even if conditions change. You traveled a long way to get here, and you should stick to your plan.
2. What is an example of traveling on a durable surface?
    a. Walking only on the designated path.
    b. Walking on the grass that borders the trail if the trail is very muddy.
    c. Taking a shortcut if you can find one because it means you will be walking less.
3. Why should you dispose of waste properly?
    a. You don't need to. Park rangers love to pick up the trash you leave behind.
    b. You should actually leave your leftovers behind, because animals will eat them. It is important to make sure they aren't hungry.
    c. So that other peoples' experiences of the park are not impacted by you leaving your waste behind.
4. How can you best follow the concept "leave what you find?"
    a. Take only a small rock or leaf to remember your trip.
    b. Take pictures, but leave any physical items where they are.
    c. Leave everything you find, unless it may be rare like an arrowhead, then it is okay to take.
5. What is not a good example of minimizing campfire impacts?
    a. Only having a campfire in a pre-existing campfire ring.
    b. Checking in with current conditions when you consider making a campfire.
    c. Building a new campfire ring in a location that has a better view.
6. What is a poor example of respecting wildlife?
    a. Building squirrel houses out of rocks so the squirrels have a place to live.
    b. Stay far away from wildlife and give them plenty of space.
    c. Reminding your grown-ups not to drive too fast in animal habitats while visiting the park.
7. How can you show consideration of other visitors?
    a. Play music on your speaker so other people at the campground can enjoy it.
    b. Wear headphones on the trail if you choose to listen to music.
    c. Make sure to yell "Hello!" to every animal you see at top volume.

Park Poetry

America's parks inspire art of all kinds. Painters, sculptors, photographers, writers, and artists of all mediums have taken inspiration from natural beauty. They have turned their inspiration into great works.

Use this space to write your own poem about the park. Think about what you have experienced or seen. Use descriptive language to create an acrostic poem. This type of poem has the first letter of each line spell out another word. Create an acrostic that spells out the word "Utah."

U ___________________________

T ___________________________

A ___________________________

H ___________________________

Under big sky

Towering rocks

All around me

Hot dry land

Up in the air

Top predator

A bird so ferocious

Hovering over its prey

Making a Difference

It is important to protect the valuable resources of the world, not just beautiful places like national parks.

How many of these things do you do at home? If you answered "no" to more than 10 items, talk to the grownups in your life to see if there are any household habits you might be able to change. Conserving our collective resources helps us all.

Yes	No	Do you…
☐	☐	turn off the water when brushing your teeth?
☐	☐	use LED light bulbs when possible?
☐	☐	use a reusable water bottle instead of disposable ones?
☐	☐	ride your bike or take the bus instead of riding in the car?
☐	☐	have a rain barrel under your roof gutters to collect rain water?
☐	☐	take quick showers?
☐	☐	avoid putting more food on your plate than you will eat?
☐	☐	take reusable lunch containers?
☐	☐	grow a garden?
☐	☐	buy items with less packaging?
☐	☐	recycle paper?
☐	☐	recycle plastic?
☐	☐	have a compost pile at home so you can make your own soil?
☐	☐	pick up trash when you see it on the trail?
☐	☐	plan a "staycation" and fly only when you have to?

# of Yes	# of No

Add up your score! Are there any "no"s that you want to turn into a yes?

Can you think of any other ways to protect our natural resources?

Catch a Fish in the Virgin River

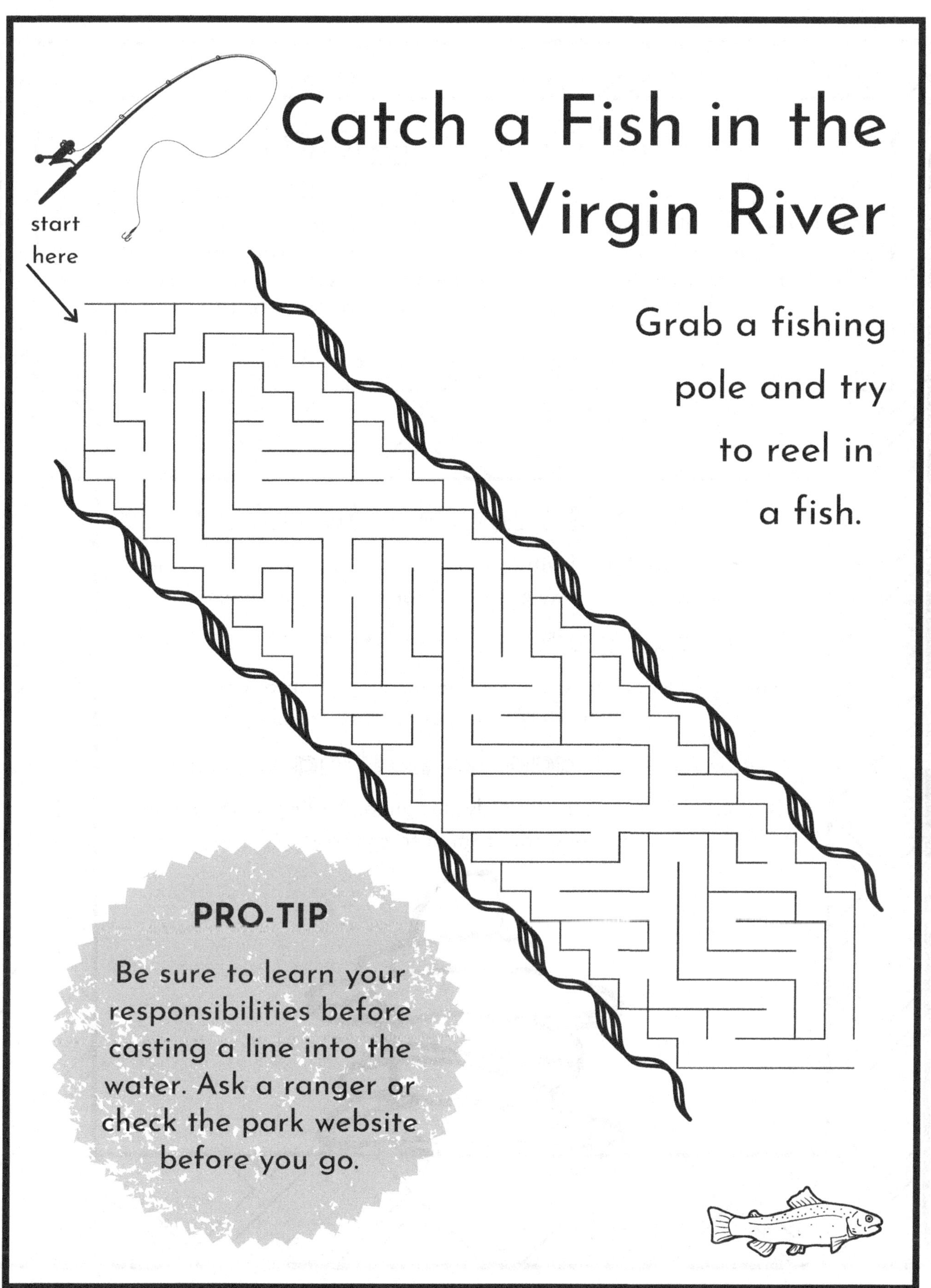

Grab a fishing pole and try to reel in a fish.

PRO-TIP

Be sure to learn your responsibilities before casting a line into the water. Ask a ranger or check the park website before you go.

Stacking Rocks

Have you ever seen stacks of rocks while hiking in national parks? Do you know what they are or what they mean? These rock piles are called cairns and often mark hiking routes in parks. Every park has a different way to maintain trails and cairns. However, they all have the same rule: If you come across a cairn, do not disturb it!

Color the cairn and the rules to remember.

1. Do not tamper with cairns.

If a cairn is tampered with or an unauthorized one is built, then future visitors may become disoriented or even lost.

2. Do not build unauthorized cairns.

Moving rocks disturbs the soil and makes the area more prone to erosion. Disturbing rocks can disturb fragile plants.

3. Do not add to existing cairns.

Authorized cairns are carefully designed. Adding to them can actually cause them to collapse.

Decoding Using American Sign Language

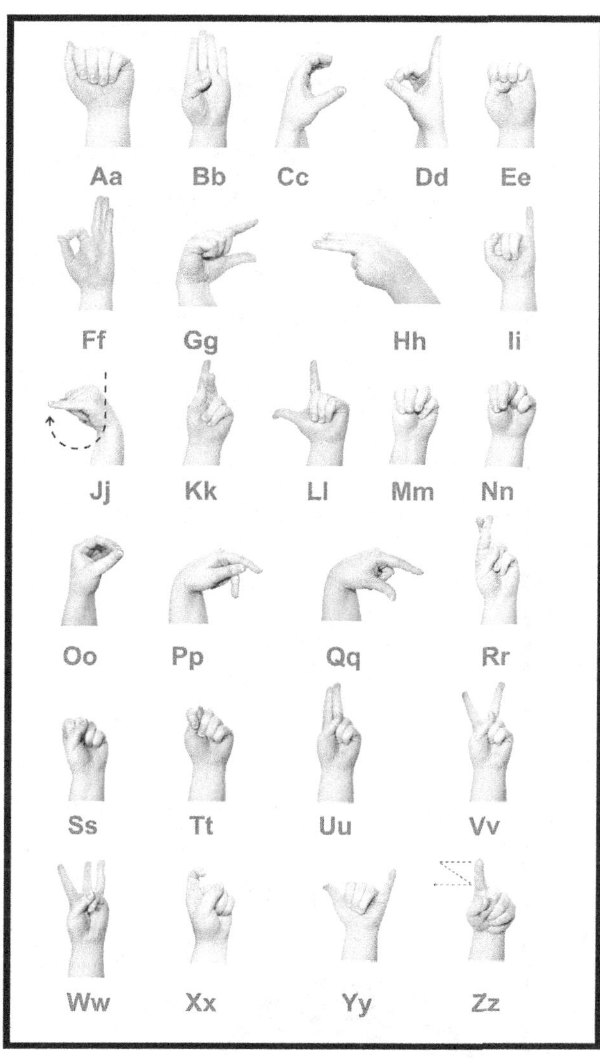

American Sign Language, also called ASL for short, is a language that many Deaf people or people who are hard of hearing use to communicate. People use ASL to communicate with their hands. Did you know people from all over the country and world travel to national parks? You may hear people speaking other languages. You might also see people using ASL. Use the American Manual Alphabet chart to decode some national parks facts.

This was the first national park to be established:

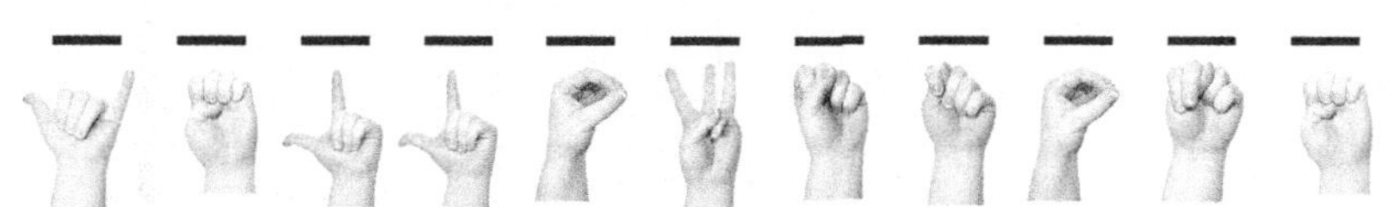

— — — — — — — — — —

This is the biggest national park in the US:

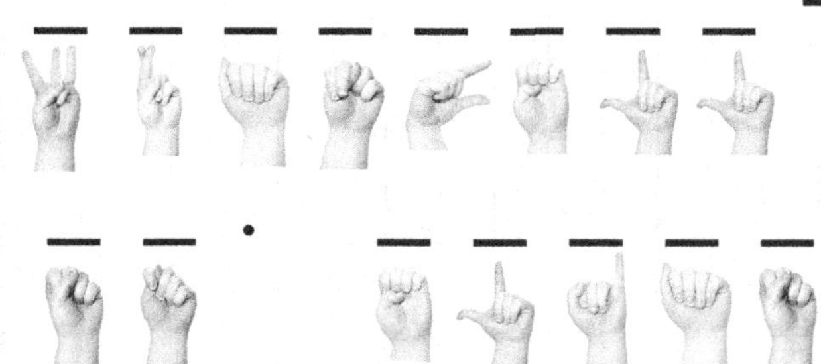

This is the most visited national park:

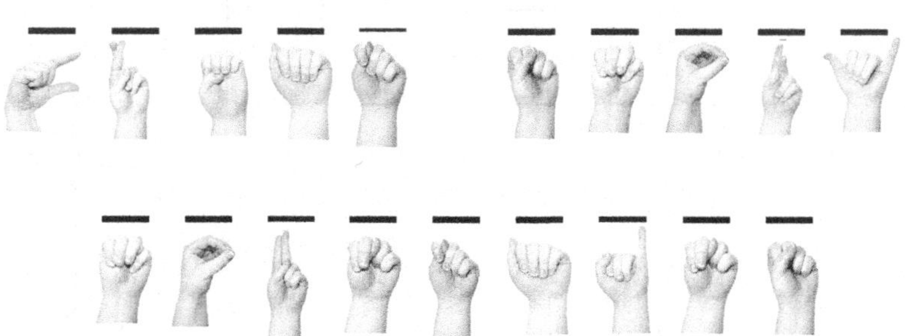

Hint: Pay close attention to the position of the thumb!

Try it! Using the chart, try to make the letters of the alphabet with your hand. What is the hardest letter to make? Can you spell out your name? Show a friend or family member and have them watch you spell out the name of the national park you are in.

Go Horseback Riding on the Hop Valley Trail

Help find the horse's lost shoe!

start
here

Butterflies of the Utah Desert

Dozens of species of butterflies and moths live in Zion National Park. Their wingspan size varies, as do the patterns on their wings. Design your own butterfly below. Make sure the wings are symmetrical, which means both sides match.

A Hike at Angels Landing

Fill in the blanks on this page without looking at the full story. Once you have each line filled out, use the words you've chosen to complete the story on the next page.

ADJECTIVE ____________________

SOMETHING TO EAT ____________________

SOMETHING TO DRINK ____________________

NOUN ____________________

ARTICLE OF CLOTHING ____________________

BODY PART ____________________

VERB ____________________

ANIMAL ____________________

SAME TYPE OF FOOD ____________________

ADJECTIVE ____________________

SAME ANIMAL ____________________

VERB THAT ENDS IN "ED" ____________________

NUMBER ____________________

A DIFFERENT NUMBER ____________________

SOMETHING THAT FLIES ____________________

LIGHT SOURCE ____________________

PLURAL NOUN ____________________

FAMILY MEMBER ____________________

YOUR NICKNAME ____________________

A Hike at Angels Landing

Use the words from the previous page to complete a silly story.

I went for a hike at Angels Landing today. In my favorite _________
ADJECTIVE

backpack, I made sure to pack a map so I wouldn't get lost. I also threw in an

extra ___________ just in case I got hungry and a bottle of ___________.
SOMETHING TO EAT   SOMETHING TO DRINK

I put on my ___________ spray, and I tied a ___________ around my
NOUN   ARTICLE OF CLOTHING

___________, in case it gets chilly. I started to _______ down the path. As
BODY PART   VERB

soon as I turned the corner, I came face to face with a(n) _________. I think
ANIMAL

it was as startled as I was! What should I do? I had to think fast! Should I

give it some of my ___________? No. I had to remember what the
SAME TYPE OF FOOD

_________ ranger told me: "If you see one, back away slowly and try not to
ADJECTIVE

scare it." Soon enough, the ___________ ___________ away. The coast
SAME ANIMAL   VERB THAT ENDS IN ED

was clear. _______ hours later, I finally got to the lookout. I felt like I could
NUMBER

see for a _______ miles. I took a picture of a _________ so I could always
A DIFFERENT NUMBER   NOUN

remember this moment. As I was putting my camera away, a ___________
SOMETHING THAT FLIES

flew by, reminding me that it was almost nighttime. I turned on my

___________ and headed back. I could hear the ___________ singing their
LIGHT SOURCE   PLURAL INSECT

evening song. Just as I was getting tired, I saw my ___________ and our tent.
FAMILY MEMBER

"Welcome back _________! How was your hike?"
NICKNAME

Connect the Dots #3

While California Condors are still rare in Zion National Park, they can sometimes be seen flying over Angels Landing. They have the largest wingspan of any other bird in North America: up to eleven feet! A wingspan is the distance from one wingtip to the other wingtip. There is a similar measurement for humans. This is called an arm span since humans don't have wings.

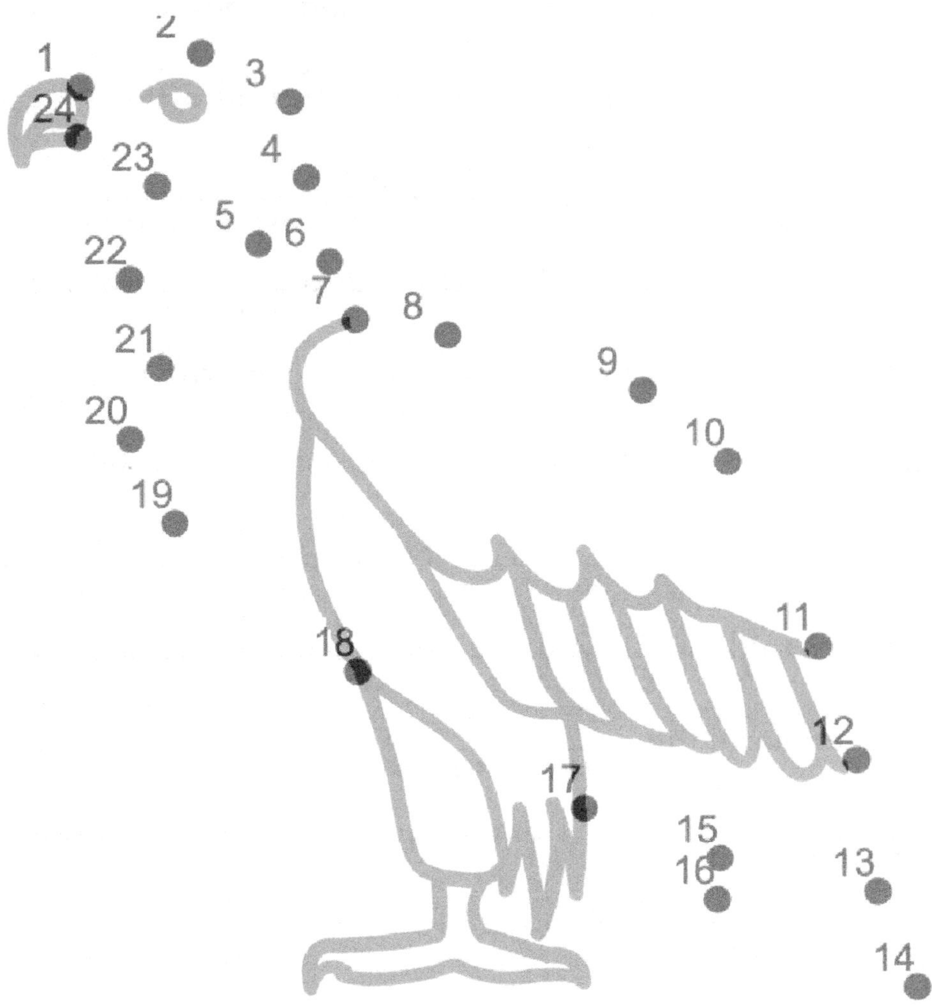

Do you know how long your arm span is? You can have a friend or family member help you measure it. Stand with your back against a wall and stretch out your arms. With a measuring tape, measure from the tip of your left middle finger to the tip of your right middle finger. How long is your arm span? Is it longer or shorter than the wingspan of a California Condor?

____

____

Let's Go Camping at Watchman Campground

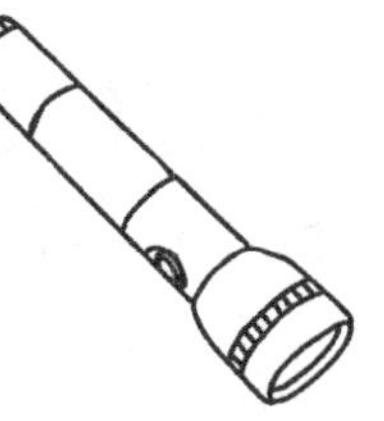

Words may be horizontal, vertical, diagonal, or they might even be backwards!

1. tent
2. camp stove
3. sleeping bag
4. bug spray
5. sunscreen
6. map
7. flashlight
8. pillow
9. lantern
10. ice
11. snacks
12. smores
13. water
14. first aid kit
15. chair
16. cards
17. books
18. games
19. trail
20. hat

```
D P P I L L O W D B T E A C I
E O A D P R E A A M B R C A N
P W C A M P S T O V E I H X G
R A H S G E L E B E E D A P S
E L B U G S P R A Y N G I E A
S I A H G C I C N N M E R C N
C W N L A F I R S K O O B F K
M T A E M I L E L H M R W L J
T A P R E A O R E S L B A A B
S M P A S R R T E N T L U S C
C E A I I R C G P E I U J H A
S S N A C K S S I M O K I L R
I J R S F O I S N J R A Q I D
C Y E T L E V E G U O R V G S
E W T A K C A B B S S O H H M
X J N F I R S T A I D K I T T
U A A E S S E N G E T P V A B
C J L I A R T D N A M A H A S
```

All in the Day of a Park Ranger

Park Rangers are hardworking individuals dedicated to protecting our parks, monuments, museums, and more. They take care of the natural and cultural resources for future generations. Rangers also help protect the visitors of the park. Their responsibilities are broad and they work both with the public and behind the scenes.

What have you seen park rangers do? Use your knowledge of the duties of park rangers to fill out a typical daily schedule, listing one activity for each hour. Feel free to make up your own, but some examples of activities are provided on the right. Read carefully! Not all the example activities are befitting a ranger.

Time	Activity		Examples
6 am	Lead a sunrise hike		• feed the migratory birds
7 am			• build trails for visitors to enjoy
8 am			• throw rocks off the side of Angels Landing
9 am			• rescue lost hikers
10 am			• study animal behavior
11 am			• record air quality data
12 pm	Enjoy a lunch break outside		• answer questions at the visitor center
1 pm			• pick wildflowers
2 pm			• pick up litter
3 pm			• share marshmallows with squirrels
4 pm	Teach visitors about the geology of the area		• repair handrails
5 pm			• lead a class on a field trip
6 pm			• catch frogs or toads and make them race
7 pm			• lead people on educational hikes
8 pm			• write articles for the park website
9 pm			• protect the river from pollution

Additional examples:
• remove non-native plants from the park
• study how climate change is affecting the park
• give a talk about mountain lions
• lead a program for campers on night skies

If you were a park ranger, which of the above tasks would you enjoy most?

____

RANGER

Fish at Zion National Park

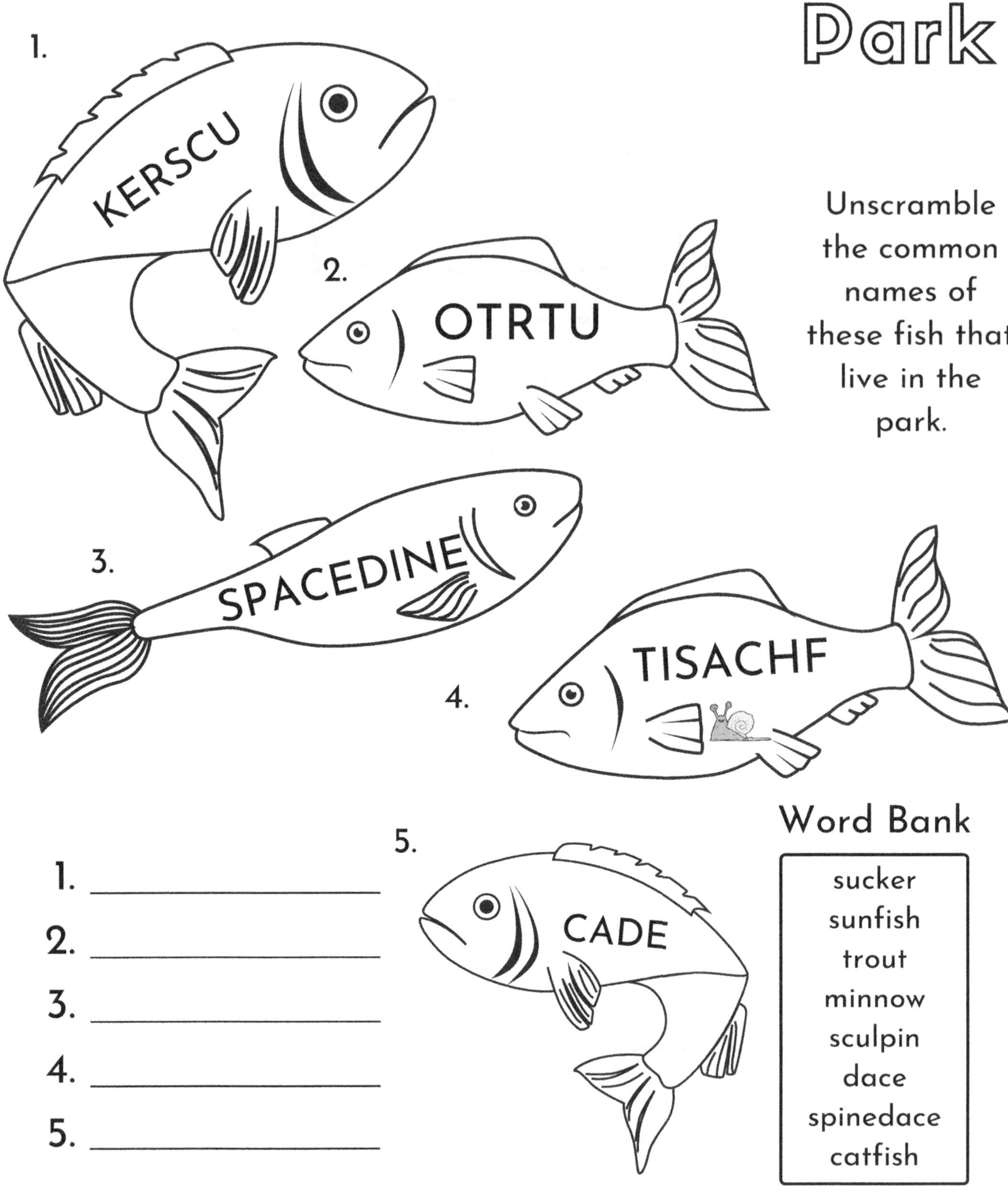

Unscramble the common names of these fish that live in the park.

1. _______________
2. _______________
3. _______________
4. _______________
5. _______________

Word Bank

sucker
sunfish
trout
minnow
sculpin
dace
spinedace
catfish

 Amphibians

Three species of toad and two species of frogs live in Zion National Park. Salamanders live there too. Frogs and toads both spend the beginning of their lives the same way - as tadpoles. Tadpoles hatch from eggs, usually in springs or pools of water.

Both frogs and toads are amphibians. Salamanders are amphibians too. Color the amphibians below.

Reflections on Special Places

National parks are special places for all sorts of reasons. Can you think of an outdoor area that is special to you? It can be a place you love because your family is from there, because it is beautiful, or because you can do your favorite things there.

What is a place (it does not have to be a national park) that is special to you?

What do national parks mean to you?

What is your favorite part of being able to enjoy the national parks around you?

Zion Weather Watch

Find a place in an open area where you can easily see the sky. Complete the activities below to provide your weather report. If you aren't in the park, you can do this activity from home.

Can you feel any wind?

What does the sky look like?

Is there anything you notice about the weather today?

What is the date?

What is the time?

Where is the sun in the sky? (rising, midpoint, falling)

What direction is the wind blowing?

Are there clouds in the sky? If so, draw them below:

63 National Parks

How many other national parks have you been to? Which one do you want to visit next? Note that if some of these parks fall on the border of more than one state, you may check it off more than once!

Alaska
- [ ] Denali National Park
- [ ] Gates of the Arctic National Park
- [ ] Glacier Bay National Park
- [ ] Katmai National Park
- [ ] Kenai Fjords National Park
- [ ] Kobuk Valley National Park
- [ ] Lake Clark National Park
- [ ] Wrangell-St. Elias National Park

American Samoa
- [ ] National Park of American Samoa

Arizona
- [ ] Grand Canyon National Park
- [ ] Petrified Forest National Park
- [ ] Saguaro National Park

Arkansas
- [ ] Hot Springs National Park

California
- [ ] Channel Islands National Park
- [ ] Death Valley National Park
- [ ] Joshua Tree National Park
- [ ] Kings Canyon National Park
- [ ] Lassen Volcanic National Park
- [ ] Pinnacles National Park
- [ ] Redwood National Park
- [ ] Sequoia National Park
- [ ] Yosemite National Park

Colorado
- [ ] Black Canyon of the Gunnison National Park
- [ ] Great Sand Dunes National Park
- [ ] Mesa Verde National Park
- [ ] Rocky Mountain National Park

Florida
- [ ] Biscayne National Park
- [ ] Dry Tortugas National Park
- [ ] Everglades National Park

Hawai'i
- [ ] Haleakalā National Park
- [ ] Hawai'i Volcanoes National Park

Idaho
- [ ] Yellowstone National Park

Kentucky
- [ ] Mammoth Cave National Park

Indiana
- [ ] Indiana Dunes National Park

Maine
- [ ] Acadia National Park

Michigan
- [ ] Isle Royale National Park

Minnesota
- [ ] Voyageurs National Park

Missouri
- [ ] Gateway Arch National Park

Montana
- [ ] Glacier National Park
- [ ] Yellowstone National Park

Nevada
- [ ] Death Valley National Park
- [ ] Great Basin National Park

New Mexico
- [ ] Carlsbad Caverns National Park
- [ ] White Sands National Park

North Dakota
- [ ] Theodore Roosevelt National Park

North Carolina
- [ ] Great Smoky Mountains National Park

Ohio
- [ ] Cuyahoga Valley National Park

Oregon
- [ ] Crater Lake National Park

South Carolina
- [ ] Congaree National Park

South Dakota
- [ ] Badlands National Park
- [ ] Wind Cave National Park

Tennessee
- [ ] Great Smoky Mountains National Park

Texas
- [ ] Big Bend National Park
- [ ] Guadalupe Mountains National Park

Utah
- [ ] Arches National Park
- [ ] Bryce Canyon National Park
- [ ] Canyonlands National Park
- [ ] Capitol Reef National Park
- [ ] Zion National Park

Virgin Islands
- [ ] Virgin Islands National Park

Virginia
- [ ] Shenandoah National Park

Washington
- [ ] Mount Rainier National Park
- [ ] North Cascades National Park
- [ ] Olympic National Park

West Virginia
- [ ] New River Gorge National Park

Wyoming
- [ ] Grand Teton National Park
- [ ] Yellowstone National Park

Other National Parks

Besides Zion National Park, there are 62 other diverse and beautiful national parks across the United States. Try your hand at this crossword. If you need help, look at the previous page for some hints.

Down

1. State where Acadia National Park is located
2. This national park has the Spanish word for turtle in it
3. Number of national parks in Alaska
5. This national park has some of the hottest temperatures in the world
6. This national park is the only one in Idaho
7. This toothsome creature can famously be found in Everglades National Park
8. Only president with a national park named for them

Across

4. This state has the most national parks.
9. This park has some of the newest land in the US, caused by volcanic eruptions.
10. This park has the deepest lake in the United States.
11. This color shows up in the name of a national park in California.
12. This national park deserves a gold medal.

Which National Park Will You Go To Next?
Word Search

1. ZION
2. BIG BEND
3. GLACIER
4. OLYMPIC
5. SEQUOIA
6. BRYCE
7. MESA VERDE
8. BISCAYNE
9. WIND CAVE
10. GREAT BASIN
11. KATMAI
12. YELLOWSTONE
13. VOYAGEURS
14. ARCHES
15. BADLANDS
16. DENALI
17. GLACIER BAY
18. HOT SPRINGS

```
F M M E S A V E R D E B N E Y
E A B I G B E N D E S A S E M
Y L I C A L O Y N E E D L T G
D M G A S S A U C N R L U E R
C E L I I T S C R E O A A K E
S N A W Y E E O I W T N A C A
G I C H A A Q C S E M D N S T
N O I Z P R U T I M R S N E B
I W E L M P O N B W E B K H A
R J R F D N I F L I H B U C S
P A B E E S A N E S O P W R I
S J A E N Y A C S I B A U A N
T C Y I A D O H H Y M E A L R
O T A T L M L E S E G R W R J
H S T O I K A T M A I R O P B
I C H U R C O L Y M P I C O U
O Y G T S D E O S B R Y C E T
W I N D C A V E I N R O H E M
```

Field Notes

Spend some time reflecting on your trip to Zion National Park. Your field notes will help you remember the things you experienced. Use the space below to write about your day.

While I was at Zion National Park...

I saw:

I heard:

I felt:

Draw a picture of your favorite thing in the park.

I wondered:

ANSWER
KEY

National Park Emblem Answers

1. This represents all plants: **Sequoia Tree**

2. This represents all animals: **Bison**

3. This represents the landscapes: **Mountains**

4. This represents the waters protected by the park service: **Water**

5. This represents the historical and archeological values: **Arrowhead**

Jumbles Answers

1. STAR GAZING

2. HIKING

3. BIRDING

4. CAMPING

5. PICNICKING

6. SIGHTSEEING

7. HORSEBACK RIDING

Take breaks to rest in the shade.

Stay hydrated by drinking lots of water.

Wear sunscreen and sun-protective clothing.

Go Birdwatching at Watchman Trail

Answers: Who Lives Here?

Below are 9 plants and animals that live in the park.
Use the word bank to fill in the clues below.

WORD BANK:

CHEATGRASS, GOPHER SNAKE, BOBCAT, CANYON WREN, MULE DEER,
PRICKLY PEAR, COTTONTAIL, OSPREY, WHIPTAIL

Find the Match!
Common Names and Latin Names

Match the common name to the scientific name for each animal. The first one is done for you. Use clues on the page before and after this one to complete the matches.

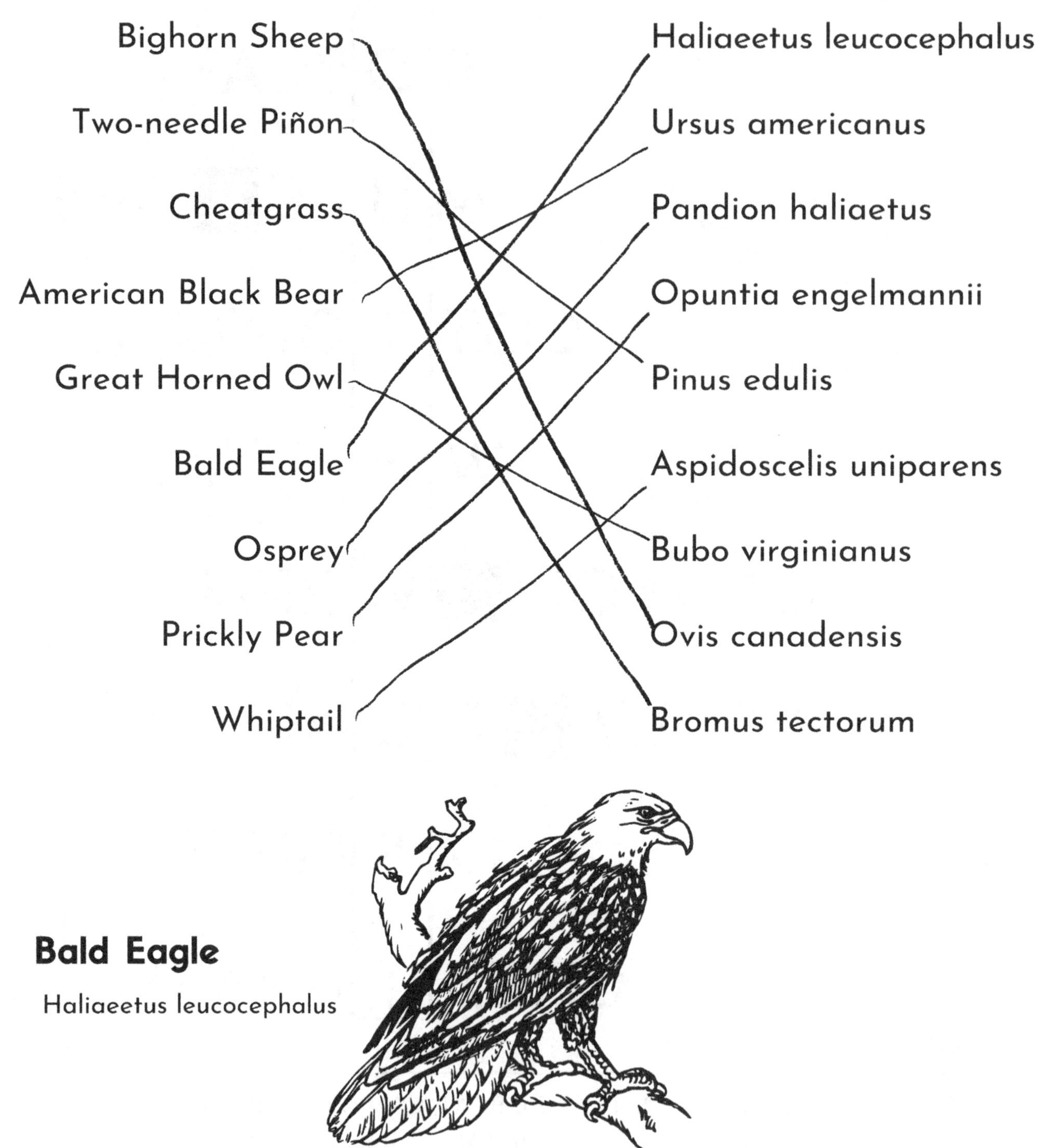

Bald Eagle

Haliaeetus leucocephalus

Answers: The Ten Essentials

Careful preparation and knowledge are key to a successful adventure into Zion National Park's backcountry.

The ten essentials are a list of things that are important to have when you go for longer hikes. If you go on a hike to the <u>backcountry</u>, it is especially important that you have everything you need in case of an emergency. If you get lost or something unforeseen happens, it is good to be prepared to survive until help finds you.

The ten essentials list was developed in the 1930s by an outdoors group called the Mountaineers. Over time and technological advancements, this list has evolved. Can you identify all the things on the current list? Circle each of the "essentials" and cross out everything that doesn't make the cut.

fire: matches, lighter, tinder, and/or stove	a pint of milk	extra money	headlamp, plus extra batteries	extra clothes
extra water	a dog	Polaroid camera	bug net	lightweight game like a deck of cards
extra food	roll of duct tape	shelter	sun protection, such as sunglasses, sun-protective clothes and sunscreen	knife, plus a gear repair kit
a mirror	navigation: map, compass, altimeter, GPS device, or satellite messenger	first aid kit	extra flip-flops	entertainment like video games or books

Backcountry - a remote undeveloped rural area.

Zion Word Search

Words may be horizontal, vertical, diagonal,
or they might be backwards!

1. Narrows
2. Kolob
3. sunset
4. rafting
5. southwest
6. Lava Point
7. flash flood
8. lodge
9. yucca
10. juniper
11. Paiute
12. Mormon
13. homestead
14. plateau
15. sandstone
16. condor
17. shuttle
18. Angels Landing

```
H M R E G N I M O Y W R M D F
L A V A P O I N T R O A O A L
O L N F P I T H F U L F S G A
S C H G O L I C E L T T U H S
L O D G E Y A T E S E I N G H
V N D S L L G T B I S N E F L
P D H O M E S T E A D G E N R O
E O M A R N O L E A E T T R O
R R P T O O T P A I U T E C O
K S Y M H E K R T N N A S A D
L G R A F E N O T S D N A S A
A O D H R F A G L K H I O P R
M I E W I A R O I O T I N I C
J U N I P E R N N A B C D G H
R M N L E R O D S A C C U Y O
A S Q U I R W E L E R A M E N
O C R T R A S O U T H W E S T
B J A C K N B R I V E R A D M
```

Answers: Find the Match!
What are Baby Animals Called?

Match the animal to its baby. The first one is done for you.

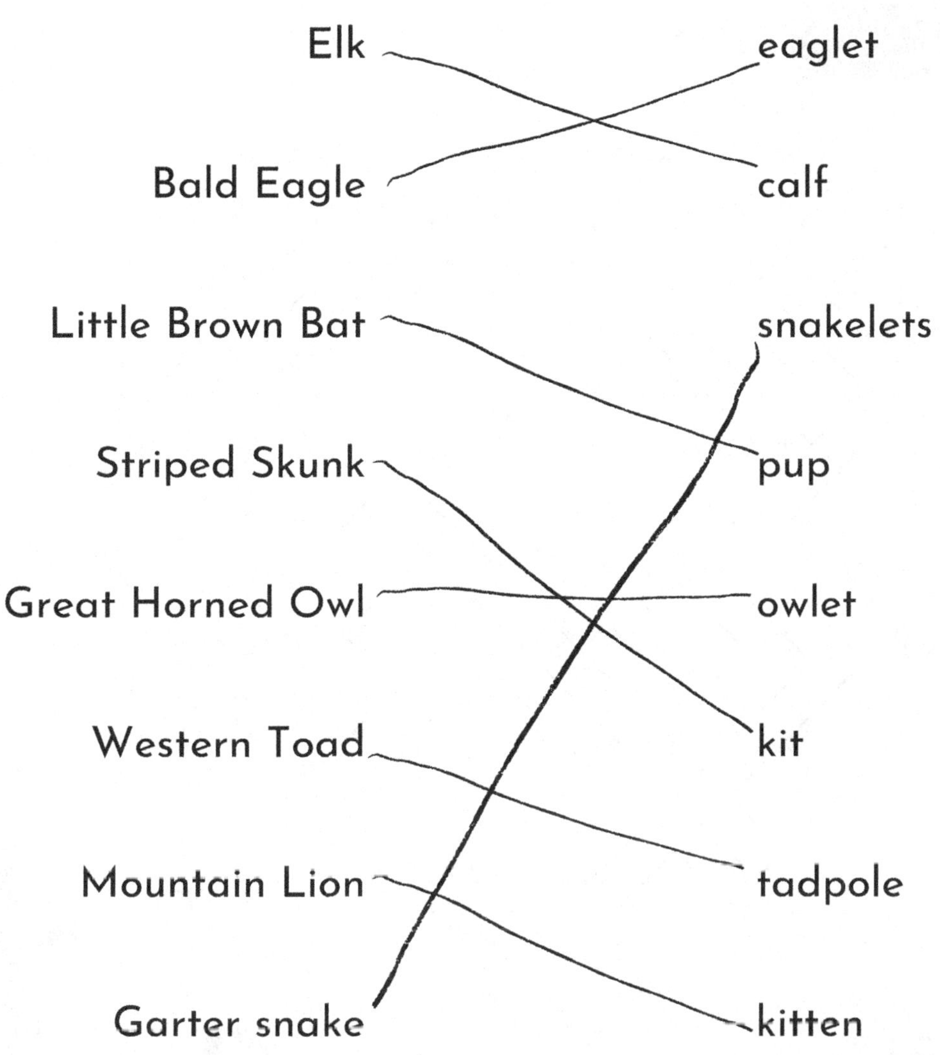

Answer: Hike to a Hoodoo

DID YOU KNOW?

Hoodoos are tall, thin rocks that protrude from the bottom of a basin. Have you seen any in the park?

Utah Word Search

Words may be horizontal, vertical, diagonal, or they might even be backwards!

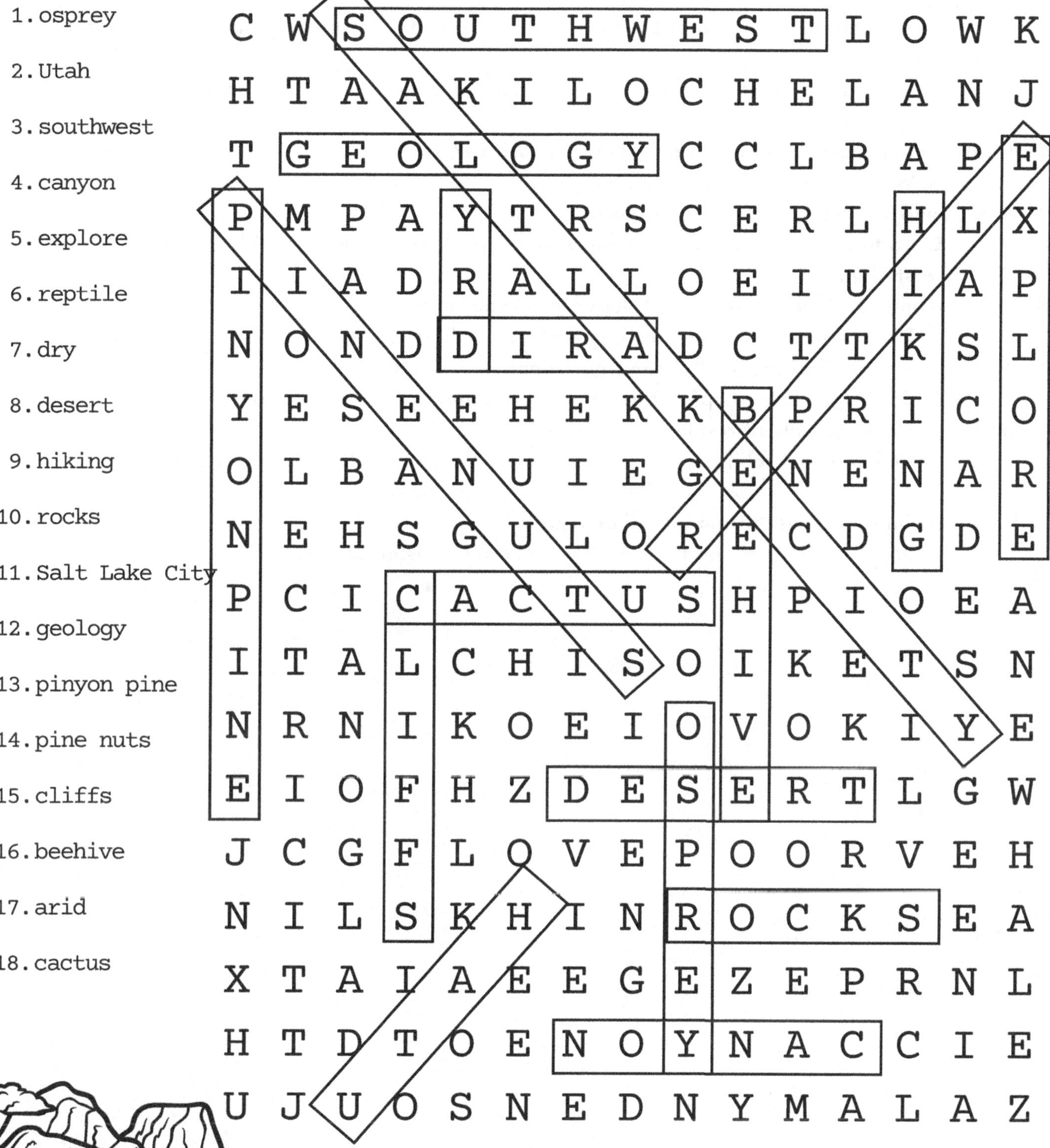

1. osprey
2. Utah
3. southwest
4. canyon
5. explore
6. reptile
7. dry
8. desert
9. hiking
10. rocks
11. Salt Lake City
12. geology
13. pinyon pine
14. pine nuts
15. cliffs
16. beehive
17. arid
18. cactus

Answers: Leave No Trace Quiz

Leave No Trace is a concept that helps people make decisions during outdoor recreation that protects the environment. There are seven principles that guide us when we spend time outdoors, whether you are in a national park or not. Are you an expert in Leave No Trace? Take this quiz and find out!

1. How can you plan ahead and prepare to ensure you have the best experience you can in the National Park?
   A. Make sure you stop by the ranger station for a map and to ask about current conditions.
2. What is an example of traveling on a durable surface?
   A. Walking only on the designated path.
3. Why should you dispose of waste properly?
   C. So that other peoples' experiences of the park are not impacted by you leaving your waste behind.
4. How can you best follow the concept "leave what you find?"
   B. Take pictures but leave any physical items where they are.
5. What is not a good example of minimizing campfire impacts?
   C. Building a new campfire ring in a location that has a better view.
6. What is a poor example of respecting wildlife?
   A. Building squirrel houses out of rocks from the river so the squirrels have a place to live.
7. How can you show consideration of other visitors?
   B. Wear headphones on the trail if you choose to listen to music.

Solution: Catch a Fish in the Virgin River

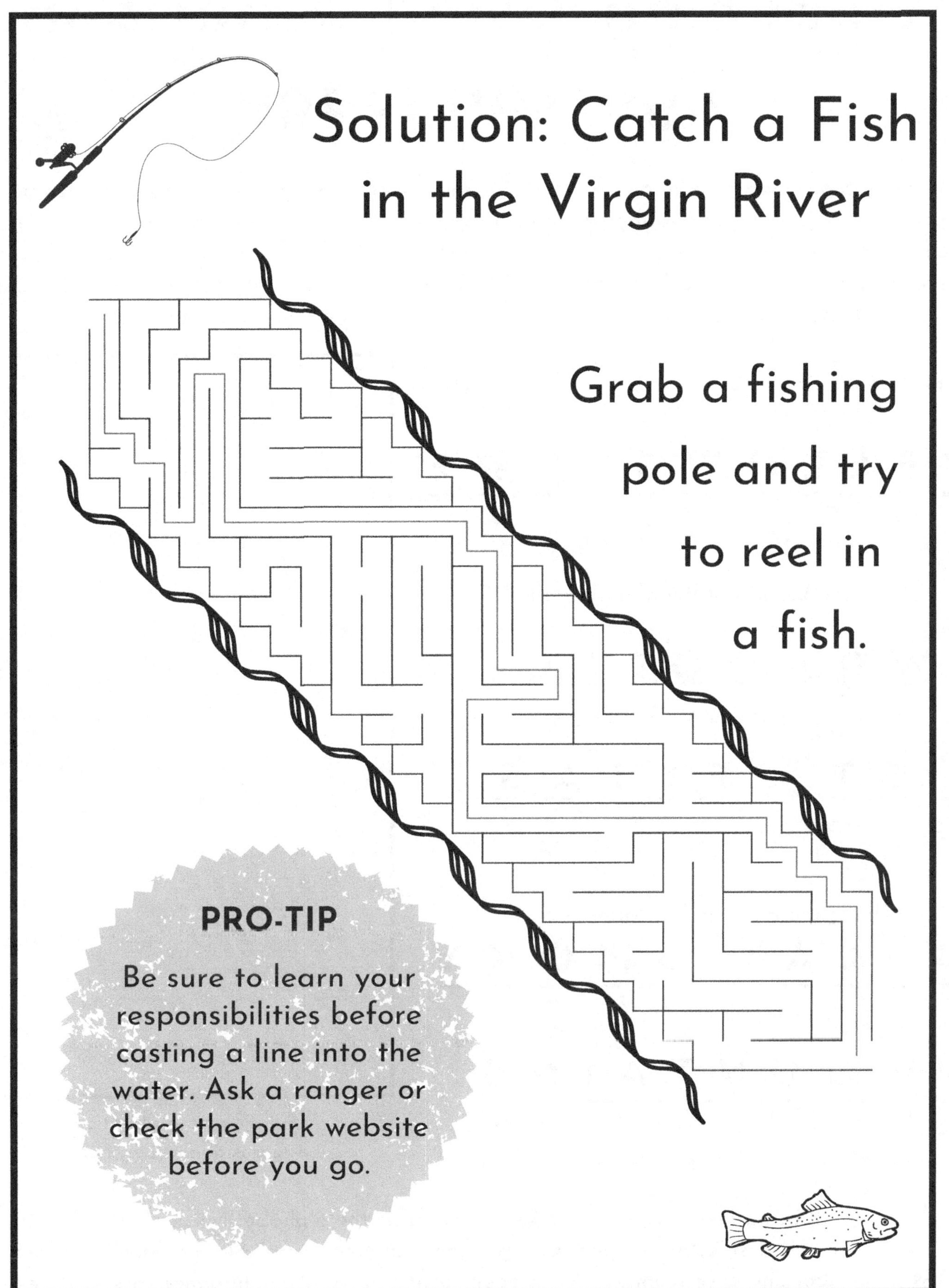

Grab a fishing pole and try to reel in a fish.

PRO-TIP

Be sure to learn your responsibilities before casting a line into the water. Ask a ranger or check the park website before you go.

Decoding Using American Sign Language

American Sign Language, also called ASL for short, is a language that many Deaf people or people who are hard of hearing use to communicate. People use ASL to communicate with their hands. Did you know people from all over the country and world travel to national parks? You may hear people speaking other languages. You might also see people using ASL. Use the American Manual Alphabet chart to decode some national parks facts.

This was the first national park to be established:

Y E L L O W S T O N E

This is the biggest national park in the US:

W R A N G E L L -
S T . E L I A S

This is the most visited national park:

G R E A T   S M O K Y
M O U N T A I N S
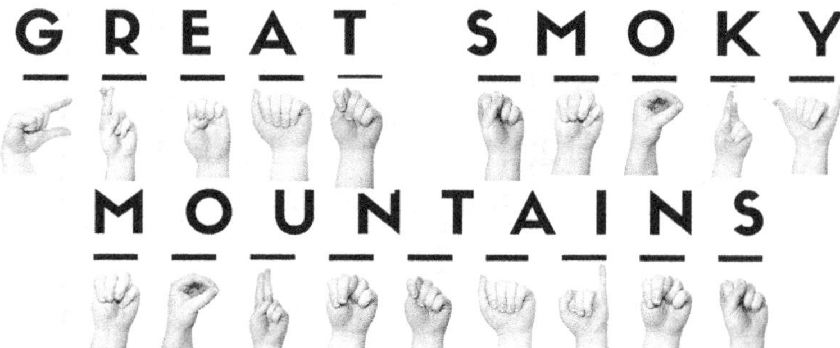

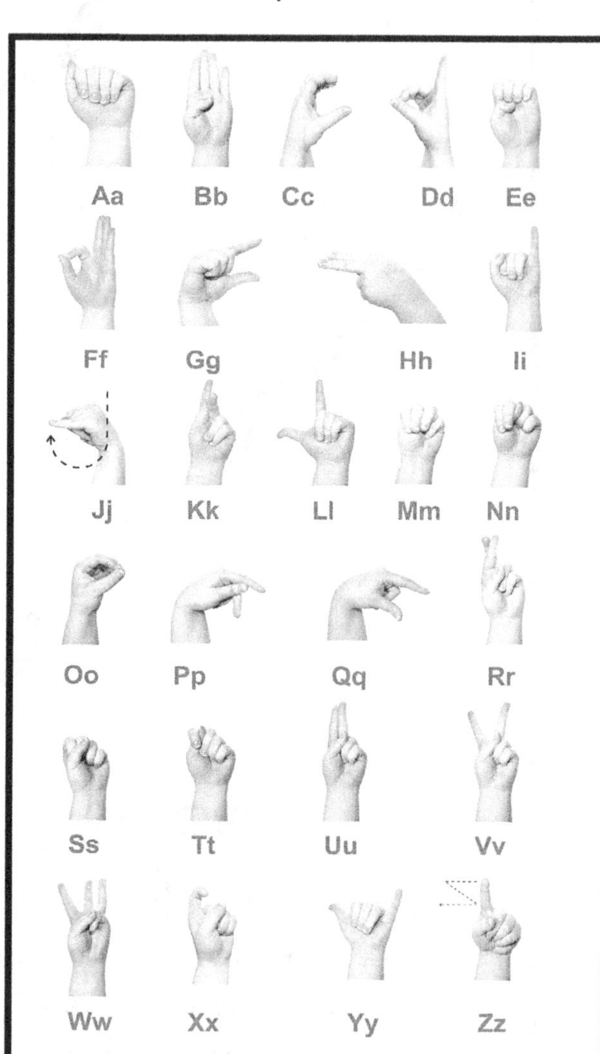

Hint: Pay close attention to the position of the thumb!

Try it! Using the chart, try to make the letters of the alphabet with your hand. What is the hardest letter to make? Can you spell out your name? Show a friend or family member and have them watch you spell out the name of the national park you are in.

Go Horseback Riding on the Hop Valley Trail

Help find the horse's lost shoe!

Answers: Let's Go Camping at Watchman Campground

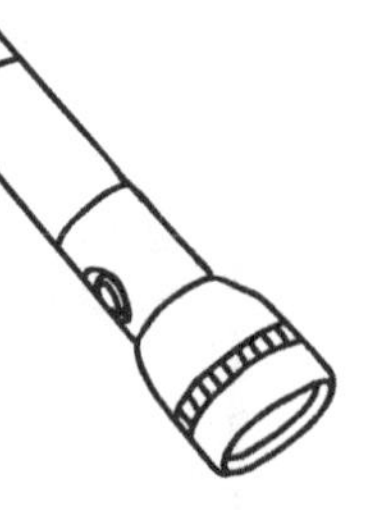

1. tent
2. camp stove
3. sleeping bag
4. bug spray
5. sunscreen
6. map
7. flashlight
8. pillow
9. lantern
10. ice
11. snacks
12. smores
13. water
14. first aid kit
15. chair
16. cards
17. books
18. games
19. trail
20. hat

D	P	P	I	L	L	O	W	D	B	T	E	A	C	I
E	O	A	D	P	R	E	A	A	M	B	R	C	A	N
P	W	C	A	M	P	S	T	O	V	E	I	H	X	G
R	A	H	S	G	E	L	E	B	E	E	D	A	P	S
E	L	B	U	G	S	P	R	A	Y	N	G	I	E	A
S	I	A	H	G	C	I	C	N	N	M	E	R	C	N
C	W	N	L	A	F	I	R	S	K	O	O	B	F	K
M	T	A	E	M	I	L	E	L	H	M	R	W	L	J
T	A	P	R	E	A	O	R	E	S	L	B	A	A	B
S	M	P	A	S	R	R	T	E	N	T	L	U	S	C
C	E	A	I	I	R	C	G	P	E	I	U	J	H	A
S	S	N	A	C	K	S	S	I	M	O	K	I	L	R
I	J	R	S	F	O	I	S	N	J	R	A	Q	I	D
C	Y	E	T	L	E	V	E	G	U	O	R	V	G	S
E	W	T	A	K	C	A	B	B	S	S	O	H	H	M
X	J	N	F	I	R	S	T	A	I	D	K	I	T	T
U	A	A	E	S	S	E	N	G	E	T	P	V	A	B
C	J	L	I	A	R	T	D	N	A	M	A	H	A	S

68

All in the Day of a Park Ranger

There are many right answers for this activity, but not all of the provided examples are good activities for a park ranger. In fact, a park ranger's job may include stopping visitors from doing some of these things.

The list below are activities that rangers do not do:

feed the migratory birds

throw rocks off the side of Angels Landing

rescue lost hikers

pick wildflowers

share marshmallows with squirrels

catch frogs or toads and make them race

Fish at Zion National Park

1. SUCKER
2. TROUT
3. SPINEDACE
4. CATFISH
5. DACE

Answers: Other National Parks

Down

1. State where Acadia National Park is located
2. This National Park has the Spanish word for turtle in it
3. Number of National Parks in Alaska
5. This National Park has some of the hottest temperatures in the world
6. This National Park is the only one in Idaho
7. This toothsome creature can famously be found in Everglades National Park
8. Only president with a national park named for them

Across

4. This state has the most National Parks
9. This park has some of the newest land in the US, caused by a volcanic eruption
10. This park has the deepest lake in the United States
11. This color shows up in the name of a National Park in California
12. This National Park deserves a gold medal

Answers: Which National Park Will You Go To Next?

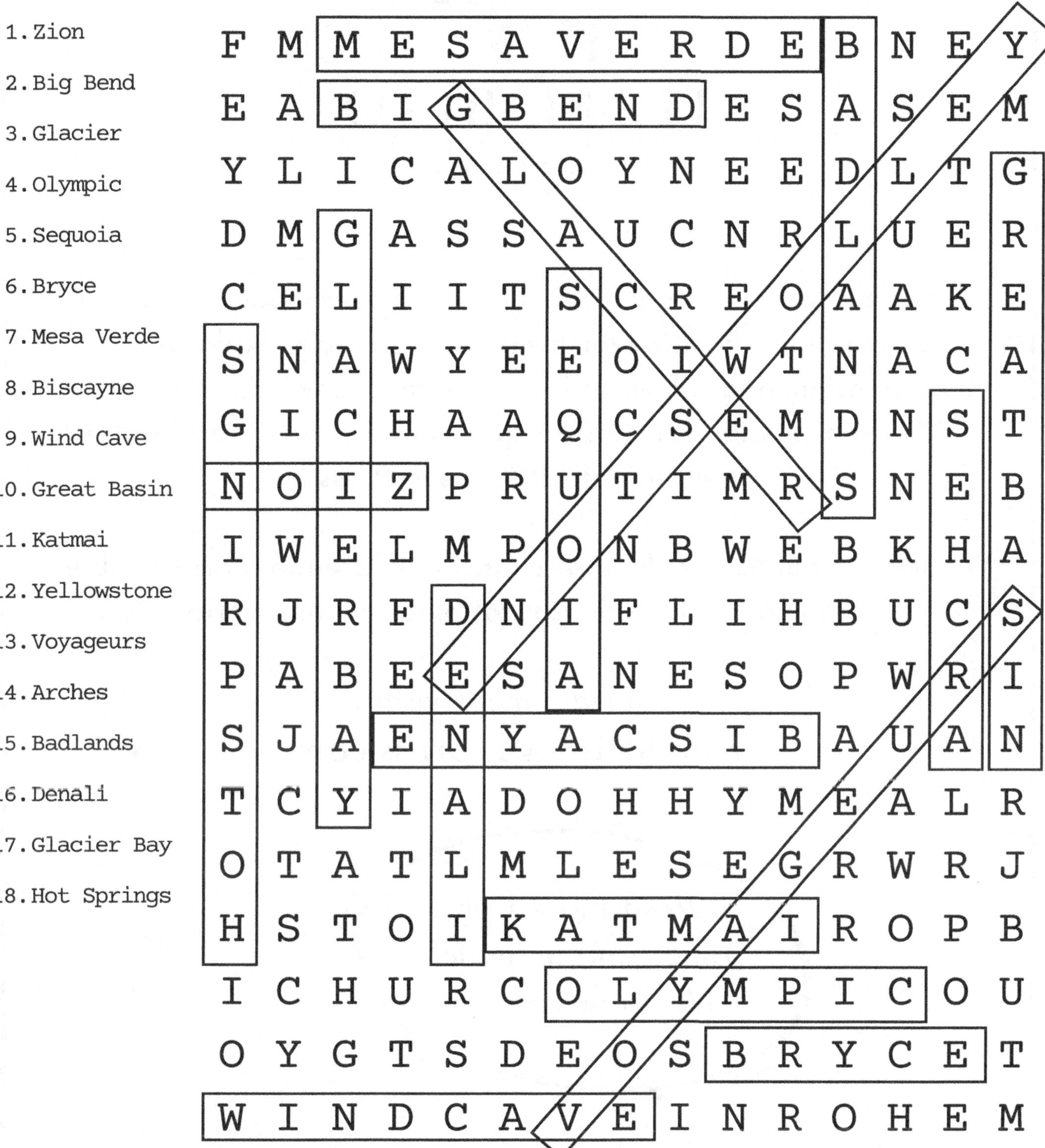

1. Zion
2. Big Bend
3. Glacier
4. Olympic
5. Sequoia
6. Bryce
7. Mesa Verde
8. Biscayne
9. Wind Cave
10. Great Basin
11. Katmai
12. Yellowstone
13. Voyageurs
14. Arches
15. Badlands
16. Denali
17. Glacier Bay
18. Hot Springs

Little Bison Press is an independent children's book publisher based in the Pacific Northwest. We promote exploration, conservation, and adventure through our books. Established in 2021, our passion for outside spaces and travel inspired the creation of Little Bison Press.

We seek to publish books that support children in learning about and caring for the natural places in our world.

To learn more, visit:
www.littlebisonpress.com

Made in United States
North Haven, CT
25 May 2024

52938329R00043